THE BOOK OF
Fairies

THE BOOK OF

Fairies

Selected and
Illustrated by

MICHAEL HAGUE

Summit Free Public Library

HarperCollins*Publishers*

To Meghan and Leigh

The Book of Fairies
Copyright © 2000 by Michael Hague
"More about Fairies" and "Notes" were written by Judy Levin.
"The Brownie o' Ferne-Den" from *Favorite Fairy Tales Told in Scotland*,
by Virginia Haviland, reprinted by permission of
Little, Brown and Co. Copyright 1963 by Virginia Haviland.
Manufactured in China.
No part of this book may be used or reproduced in any manner whatsoever
without written permission except in the case of brief quotations embodied
in critical articles and reviews. For information address
HarperCollins Children's Books, a division of HarperCollins Publishers,
1350 Avenue of the Americas, New York, NY 10019.
All rights reserved.
www.harpercollinschildrens.com

Library of Congress Cataloging-in-Publication Data
The book of fairies / selected and illustrated by Michael Hague.
p. cm.
Summary: A collection of stories and poems about fairies,
including an excerpt from James Barrie's "Peter Pan in Kensington Gardens,"
Hans Christian Andersen's "Thumbelina," and Christina Rossetti's "Goblin Market."
ISBN-10: 0-688-10881-4 (trade bdg.) — ISBN-13: 978-0-688-10881-6 (trade bdg.)
ISBN-10: 0-06-089187-4 (pbk.) — ISBN-13: 978-0-06-089187-9 (pbk.)
I. Fairies—Literary collections.   [I. Fairies—Literary collections.]   I. Hague, Michael.
PZ5.B6425 2000   808.8'0375—dc21   99-32512

First Edition

Contents

Lock-out Time

from Peter Pan in Kensington Gardens *by J. M. Barrie*

*I*T IS FRIGHTFULLY DIFFICULT to know much about the fairies, and almost the only thing known for certain is that there are fairies wherever there are children. Long ago children were forbidden the Gardens, and at that time there was not a fairy in the place; then the children were admitted, and the fairies came trooping in that very evening. They can't resist following the children, but you seldom see them, partly because they live in the daytime behind the railings, where you are not allowed to go, and also partly because they are so cunning. They are not a bit cunning after Lock-out, but until Lock-out, my word!

When you were a bird you knew the fairies pretty well, and you remember a good deal about them in your babyhood, which it is a great pity you can't write down, for gradually you forget, and I have heard of children who declared that they had never once seen a fairy. Very likely if they said this in the Kensington Gardens, they were standing looking at a fairy all the time. The reason they were cheated was that she pretended to be something else. This is one of their best tricks. They usually pretend to be flowers, because the court sits in the Fairies' Basin, and there are so many flowers there, and all along the Baby Walk, that a flower is the thing least likely to attract attention. They dress exactly like flowers, and change with the seasons, putting on white when lilies are in and blue for bluebells, and so on. They like crocus and hyacinth time best of all, as they are partial to a bit of color, but tulips (except white ones, which are the fairy cradles) they consider garish, and they sometimes put off dressing like tulips for days, so that the beginning of the tulip weeks is almost the best time to catch them.

When they think you are not looking they skip along pretty lively, but if you look, and they fear there is no time to hide, they stand quite still pretending to be flowers. Then, after you have passed without knowing that they were fairies, they rush home and tell their mothers they have had such an adventure. The Fairy Basin, you remember, is all covered with ground ivy (from which they make their castor oil), with flowers growing in it here and there. Most of them really are flowers, but some of them are fairies. You never can be sure of them, but a good plan is to walk by looking the other way, and then turn round sharply. Another good plan, which David and I sometimes follow, is to stare them down. After a long time they can't help winking, and then you know for certain that they are fairies.

There are also numbers of them along the Baby Walk, which is a famous gentle place, as spots frequented by fairies are called. Once twenty-four of them had an extraordinary adventure. They were a girls' school out for a walk with the governess, and all wearing hyacinth gowns, when she suddenly put her finger to her mouth, and then they all stood still on an empty bed and pretended to be hyacinths. Unfortunately, what the governess had heard was two gardeners coming to plant new flowers in that very bed. They were wheeling a handcart with the flowers in it, and were quite surprised to find the bed occupied. "Pity to lift them hyacinths," said the one man. "Duke's orders," replied the other, and, having emptied the cart, they dug up the boarding school and put the poor, terrified things in it in five rows. Of course, neither the governess nor the girls dare let on that they were fairies, so they were carted far away to a potting shed, out of which they escaped in the night without their shoes, but there was a great row about it among the parents, and the school was ruined.

As for their houses, it is no use looking for them, because they are the exact opposite of our houses. You can see our houses by day but you can't see them by dark. Well, you can see their houses by dark, but you can't see them by day, for they are the color of night, and I never heard of anyone yet who could see night in the daytime. This does not mean that they are black, for night has its colors just as day has, but ever so much brighter. Their blues and reds and greens are like ours with a light behind them. The palace is entirely built of many-colored glasses, and it is quite the loveliest of all royal residences, but the queen sometimes complains because the common people will peep in to see what she is doing. They are very inquisitive folk, and press quite hard against the glass, and that is why their noses are mostly snubby. The streets are miles long and very twisty, and have paths on each side made of bright worsted. The birds used to steal the worsted for their nests, but a policeman has been appointed to hold on at the other end.

One of the great differences between the fairies and us is that they never do anything useful. When the first baby laughed for the first time, his laugh broke into a million pieces, and they all went skipping about. That was the beginning of fairies. They look tremendously busy, you know, as if they had not a moment

to spare, but if you were to ask them what they are doing, they could not tell you in the least. They are frightfully ignorant, and everything they do is make-believe. They have a postman, but he never calls except at Christmas with his little box, and though they have beautiful schools, nothing is taught in them; the youngest child being chief person is always elected mistress, and when she has called the roll, they all go out for a walk and never come back. It is a very noticeable thing that, in fairy families, the youngest is always chief person, and usually becomes a prince or princess; and children remember this, and think it must be so among humans also, and that is why they are often made uneasy when they come upon their mother furtively putting new frills on the basinette.

You have probably observed that your baby sister wants to do all sorts of things that your mother and her nurse want her not to do—to stand up at sitting-down time, and to sit down at stand-up time, for instance, or to wake up when she should fall asleep, or to crawl on the floor when she is wearing her best frock, and so on, and perhaps you put this down to naughtiness. But it is not; it simply means that she is doing as she has seen the fairies do; she begins by following their ways, and it takes about two years to get her into the human ways. Her fits of passion, which are awful to behold, and are usually called teething, are no such thing; they are her natural exasperation, because we don't understand her, though she is talking an intelligible language. She is talking fairy. The reason mothers and nurses know what her remarks mean, before other people know, as that "Guch" means "Give it to me at once," while "Wa" is "Why do you wear such a funny hat?" is because, mixing so much with babies, they have picked up a little of the fairy language.

Of late David has been thinking back hard about the fairy tongue, with his hands clutching his temples, and he has remembered a number of their phrases, which I shall tell you someday if I don't forget. He had heard them in the days when he was a thrush, and though I suggested to him that perhaps it is really bird language he is remembering, he says not, for these phrases are about fun and adventures, and the birds talked of nothing but nest building. He distinctly remembers that the birds used to go from spot to spot like ladies at shop windows, looking at the different nests and saying, "Not my color, my dear," and "How would that do with a soft lining?" and "But will it wear?" and "What hideous trimming!" and so on.

The fairies are exquisite dancers, and that is why one of the first things the baby does is to sign to you to dance to him and then to cry when you do it. They hold their great balls in the open air, in what is called a fairy ring. For weeks afterwards you can see the ring on the grass. It is not there when they begin, but they make it by waltzing round and round. Sometimes you will find mushrooms inside the ring, and these are fairy chairs that the servants have forgotten to clear away. The chairs and the rings are the only telltale marks these little people leave behind them, and they would remove even these were they not so fond of dancing that they toe it till the very moment of the opening of the gates. David and I once found a fairy ring quite warm.

But there is also a way of finding out about the ball before it takes place. You know the boards which tell at what time the Gardens are to close today. Well, these tricky fairies sometimes slyly change the board on a ball night, so that it says the Gardens are to close at six-thirty, for instance, instead of at seven. This enables them to get begun half an hour earlier.

If on such a night we could remain behind in the Gardens, as the famous Maimie Mannering did, we might see delicious sights; hundreds of lovely fairies hastening to the ball, the married ones wearing their wedding rings round their waists; the gentlemen, all in uniform, holding up the ladies' trains, and linkmen running in front carrying winter cherries, which are the fairy lanterns; the cloak-room where they put on their silver slippers and get a ticket for their wraps; the flowers streaming up from the Baby Walk to look on, and always welcome because they can lend a pin; the supper table, with Queen Mab at the head of it, and behind her chair the Lord Chamberlain, who carries a dandelion on which he blows when her Majesty wants to know the time.

The tablecloth varies according to the seasons, and in May it is made of chestnut blossom. The way the fairy servants do is this: The men, scores of them, climb up the trees and shake the branches, and the blossom falls like snow. Then the lady servants sweep it together by whisking their skirts until it is exactly like a tablecloth, and that is how they get their tablecloth.

There is bread-and-butter to begin with, of the size of a three-penny bit; and cakes to end with, and they are so small that they have no crumbs. The fairies sit round on mushrooms, and at first they are well-behaved and always cough off the table, and so on, but after a bit they are not so well-behaved and stick their fingers into the butter, which is got from the roots of old trees, and the really horrid ones crawl over the tablecloth chasing sugar or other delicacies with their tongues. When the Queen sees them doing this she signs to the servants to wash up and put away, and then everybody adjourns to the dance, the Queen walking in front while the Lord Chamberlain walks behind her, carrying two little pots, one of which contains the juice of wallflower and the other the juice of Solomon's seals. Wallflower juice is good for reviving dancers who fall to the ground in a fit, and Solomon's seals juice is for bruises. They bruise very easily, and when Peter plays faster and faster they foot it till they fall down in fits. For, as you know without my telling you, Peter Pan is the fairies' orchestra. He sits in the middle of the ring, and they would never dream of having a smart dance nowadays without him. "P.P." is written on the corner of the invitation cards sent out by all really good families.

Thumbelina

by Hans Christian Andersen

THERE WAS ONCE a woman who wanted to have quite a tiny, little child, but she did not know where to get one from. So one day she went to an old Witch and said to her: "I should so much like to have a tiny, little child; can you tell me where I can get one?"

"Oh, we have just got one ready!" said the Witch. "Here is a barleycorn for you, but it's not the kind the farmer sows in his field, or feeds the cocks and hens with, I can tell you. Put it in a flowerpot, and then you will see something happen."

"Oh, thank you!" said the woman, and gave the Witch a shilling, for that was what it cost. Then she went home and planted the barleycorn; immediately there grew out of it a large and beautiful flower, which looked like a tulip, but the petals were tightly closed as if it were still only a bud.

"What a beautiful flower!" exclaimed the woman, and she kissed the red and yellow petals; but as she kissed them the flower burst open. It was a real tulip, such as one can see any day; but in the middle of the blossom, on the green velvety petals, sat a little girl, quite tiny, trim, and pretty. She was scarcely half a thumb in height; so they called her Thumbelina. An elegant polished walnut shell served Thumbelina as a cradle, the blue petals of a violet were her mattress, and a rose leaf her coverlet. There she lay at night, but in the daytime she used to play about on the table; here the woman had put a bowl, surrounded by a ring of flowers, with their stalks in water, in the middle of which floated a great tulip petal, and on this Thumbelina sat, and sailed from one side of the bowl to the other, rowing herself with two white horsehairs for oars. It was such a pretty sight! She could sing, too, with a voice more soft and sweet than had ever been heard before.

One night, when she was lying in her pretty little bed, an old toad crept in through a broken pane in the window. She was very ugly, clumsy, and clammy; she hopped on to the table where Thumbelina lay asleep under the red rose leaf.

"This would make a beautiful wife for my son," said the toad, taking up the walnut shell, with Thumbelina inside, and hopping with it through the window into the garden.

There flowed a great wide stream, with slippery and marshy banks; here the toad lived with her son. Ugh! How ugly and clammy he was, just like his mother! "Croak, croak, croak!" was all he could say when he saw the pretty little girl in the walnut shell.

"Don't talk so loud, or you'll wake her," said the old toad. "She might escape us even now; she is as light as a feather. We will put her at once on a broad water-lily leaf in the stream. That will be quite an island for her; she is so small and light. She can't run away from us there, whilst we are preparing the guest chamber under the marsh where she shall live."

Outside in the brook grew many water lilies, with broad green leaves, which looked as if they were swimming about on the water. The leaf farthest away was the largest, and to this the old toad swam with Thumbelina in her walnut shell.

The tiny Thumbelina woke up very early in the morning, and when she saw where she was she began to cry bitterly; for on every side of the great green leaf was water, and she could not get to the land.

The old toad was down under the marsh, decorating her room with rushes and yellow marigold leaves, to make it very grand for her new daughter-in-law; then she swam out with her ugly son to the leaf where Thumbelina lay. She wanted to fetch the pretty cradle to put it into her room before Thumbelina herself came there. The old toad bowed low in the water before her, and said: "Here is my son; you shall marry him, and live in great magnificence down under the marsh."

"Croak, croak, croak!" was all that the son could say. Then they took the neat little cradle and swam away with it; but Thumbelina sat alone on the great green leaf and wept, for she did not want to live with the clammy toad, or marry her ugly son. The little fishes swimming about under the water had seen the toad quite plainly, and heard what she had said; so they put up their heads to see the little girl. When they saw her, they thought her so pretty that they were very sorry she should go down with the ugly toad to live. No; that must not happen. They assembled in the water round the green stalk which supported the leaf on which she was sitting, and nibbled the stem in two. Away floated the leaf down the stream, bearing Thumbelina far beyond the reach of the toad.

On she sailed past several towns, and the little birds sitting in the bushes saw her, and sang, "What a pretty little girl!" The leaf floated farther and farther away; thus Thumbelina left her native land.

A beautiful little white butterfly fluttered above her, and at last settled on the leaf. Thumbelina pleased him, and she, too, was delighted, for now the toads could not reach her, and it was so beautiful where she was traveling; the sun

shone on the water and made it sparkle like the brightest silver. She took off her sash, and tied one end round the butterfly; the other end she fastened to the leaf, so that now it glided along with her faster than ever.

A great cockchafer came flying past; he caught sight of Thumbelina, and in a moment had put his arms round her slender waist, and had flown off with her to a tree. The green leaf floated away down the stream, and the butterfly with it, for he was fastened to the leaf and could not get loose from it. Oh, dear! How terrified poor little Thumbelina was when the cockchafer flew off with her to the tree! But she was especially distressed on the beautiful white butterfly's account, as she had tied him fast, so that if he could not get away he must starve to death. But the cockchafer did not trouble himself about that; he sat down with her on a large green leaf, gave her the honey out of the flowers to eat, and told her that she was very pretty, although she wasn't in the least like a cockchafer. Later on, all the other cockchafers who lived in the same tree came to pay calls; they examined Thumbelina closely, and remarked, "Why, she has only two legs! How very miserable!"

"She has no feelers!" cried another.

"How ugly she is!" said all the lady chafers—and yet Thumbelina was really very pretty.

The cockchafer who had stolen her knew this very well; but when he heard all the ladies saying she was ugly, he began to think so too, and would not keep her; she might go wherever she liked. So he flew down from the tree with her and put her on a daisy. There she sat and wept, because she was so ugly that the cockchafer would have nothing to do with her; and yet she was the most beautiful creature imaginable, so soft and delicate, like the loveliest rose leaf.

The whole summer poor little Thumbelina lived alone in the great wood. She plaited a bed for herself of blades of grass, and hung it up under a clover-leaf, so that she was protected from the rain; she gathered honey from the flowers for food, and drank the dew on the leaves every morning. Thus the summer

and autumn passed, but then came winter—the long, cold winter. All the birds who had sung so sweetly about her had flown away; the trees shed their leaves, the flowers died; the great cloverleaf under which she had lived curled up, and nothing remained of it but the withered stalk. She was terribly cold, for her clothes were ragged, and she herself was so small and thin. Poor little Thumbelina! She would surely be frozen to death. It began to snow, and every snowflake that fell on her was to her as a whole shovelful thrown on one of us, for we are so big, and she was only an inch high. She wrapped herself round in a dead leaf, but it was torn in the middle and gave her no warmth; she was trembling with cold.

Just outside the wood where she was now living lay a great cornfield. But the corn had been gone a long time; only the dry, bare stubble was left standing in the frozen ground. This made a forest for her to wander about in. All at once she came across the door of a field mouse, who had a little house in an old tree. There the mouse lived warm and snug, with a storeroom full of corn, a splendid kitchen and dining room. Poor little Thumbelina went up to the door and begged for a little piece of barley, for she had not had anything to eat for the last two days.

"Poor little creature!" said the field mouse, for she was a kindhearted old thing at the bottom. "Come into my warm room and have some dinner with me."

As Thumbelina pleased her, she said: "As far as I am concerned you may spend the winter with me; but you must keep my room clean and tidy, and tell me stories, for I like that very much."

And Thumbelina did all that the kind old field mouse asked, and did it remarkably well too.

"Now I am expecting a visitor," said the field mouse; "my neighbor comes to call on me once a week. He is in better circumstances than I am, has great, big rooms, and wears a fine black-velvet coat. If you could only marry him, you would be well provided for. But he is blind. You must tell him all the prettiest stories you know."

But Thumbelina did not trouble her head about him, for he was only a mole. He came and paid them a visit in his black-velvet coat.

"He is so rich and so accomplished," the field mouse told her. "His house is twenty times larger than mine; he possesses great knowledge, but he cannot bear the sun and the beautiful flowers, and speaks slightingly of them, for he has never seen them."

Thumbelina had to sing to him, so she sang "Lady-bird lady-bird, fly away home!" and other songs so prettily that the mole fell in love with her; but he did not say anything. He was a very cautious man. A short time before, he had dug a long passage through the ground from his own house to that of his neighbor; in this he gave the field mouse and Thumbelina permission to walk as often as they liked. But he begged them not to be afraid of the dead bird that lay in the passage: it was a real bird with a beak and feathers, and must have died a little time ago, and now lay buried just where he had made his tunnel. The mole took a piece of rotten wood in his mouth, for that glows like fire in the dark, and went in front, lighting them through the long dark passage. When they came to the place where the dead bird lay, the mole put his broad nose against the ceiling and pushed a hole through, so that the daylight could shine down. In the middle of the path lay a dead swallow, his pretty wings pressed close to his sides, his claws and head drawn under his feathers; the poor bird had evidently died of cold. Thumbelina was very sorry, for she was very fond of all little birds; they had sung and twittered so beautifully to her all through the summer. But the mole kicked him with his bandy legs and said:

"Now he can't sing anymore! It must be very miserable to be a little bird! I'm thankful that none of my little children are; birds always starve in winter."

"Yes, you speak like a sensible man," said the field mouse. "What has a bird, in spite of all his singing, in the wintertime? He must starve and freeze, and that must be very pleasant for him, I must say!"

Thumbelina did not say anything; but when the other two had passed on she bent down to the bird, brushed aside the feathers from his head, and kissed his closed eyes gently. "Perhaps it was he that sang to me so prettily in the summer," she thought. "How much pleasure he did give me, dear little bird!"

The mole closed up the hole again which let in the light, and then escorted the ladies home. But Thumbelina could not sleep that night; so she got out of bed, and plaited a great big blanket of straw, and carried it off, and spread it over the dead bird, and piled upon it thistledown as soft as cotton wool, which she had found in the field mouse's room, so that the poor little thing should lie warmly buried.

"Farewell, pretty little bird!" she said. "Farewell, and thank you for your beautiful songs in the summer, when the trees were green, and the sun shone down warmly on us!" Then she laid her head against the bird's heart. But the bird was not dead: he had been frozen, but now that she had warmed him, he was coming to life again.

In autumn the swallows fly away to foreign lands; but there are some who are late in starting, and then they get so cold that they drop down as if dead, and the snow comes and covers them over.

Thumbelina trembled, she was so frightened; for the bird was very large in comparison with herself—only an inch high. But she took courage, piled up the down more closely over the poor swallow, fetched her own coverlet and laid it over his head.

Next night she crept out again to him. There he was alive, but very weak; he could only open his eyes for a moment and look at Thumbelina, who was standing in front of him with a piece of rotten wood in her hand, for she had no other lantern.

"Thank you, pretty little child!" said the swallow to her. "I am so beautifully warm! Soon I shall regain my strength, and then I shall be able to fly out again into the warm sunshine."

"Oh!" she said. "It is very cold outside; it is snowing and freezing! Stay in your warm bed; I will take care of you!"

Then she brought him water in a petal, which he drank, after which he related to her how he had torn one of his wings on a bramble, so that he could

not fly as fast as the other swallows, who had flown far away to warmer lands. So at last he had dropped down exhausted, and then he could remember no more. The whole winter he remained down there, and Thumbelina looked after him and nursed him tenderly. Neither the mole nor the field mouse learnt anything of this, for they could not bear the poor swallow.

When the spring came, and the sun warmed the earth again, the swallow said farewell to Thumbelina, who opened the hole in the roof for him which the mole had made. The sun shone brightly down upon her, and the swallow asked her if she would go with him; she could sit upon his back. Thumbelina wanted very much to fly far away into the green wood, but she knew that the old field mouse would be sad if she ran away. "No, I mustn't come!" she said.

"Farewell, dear good little girl!" said the swallow, and flew off into the sunshine. Thumbelina gazed after him with the tears standing in her eyes, for she was very fond of the swallow.

"Tweet, tweet!" sang the bird, and flew into the green wood. Thumbelina was very unhappy. She was not allowed to go out into the warm sunshine. The corn which had been sowed in the field over the field mouse's home grew up high into the air, and made a thick forest for the poor little girl, who was only an inch high.

"Now you are to be a bride, Thumbelina," said the field mouse, "for our neighbor has proposed for you! What a piece of fortune for a poor child like you! Now you must set to work at your linen for your dowry, for nothing must be lacking if you are to become the wife of our neighbor, the mole!"

Thumbelina had to spin all day long, and every evening the mole visited her, and told her that when the summer was over the sun would not shine so hot; now it was burning the earth as hard as a stone. Yes, when the summer had passed, they would keep the wedding.

But she was not at all pleased about it, for she did not like the stupid mole. Every morning when the sun was rising, and every evening when it was setting, she would steal out of the house door, and when the breeze parted the ears of corn so that she could see the blue sky through them, she thought how bright and beautiful it must be outside, and longed to see her dear swallow again. But he never came; no doubt he had flown away far into the great green wood.

By the autumn Thumbelina had finished the dowry.

"In four weeks you will be married!" said the field mouse. "Don't be obsti-nate, or I shall bite you with my sharp white teeth! You will get a fine husband! The King himself has not such a velvet coat. His storeroom and cellar are full, and you should be thankful for that."

Well, the wedding day arrived. The mole had come to fetch Thumbelina to live with him deep down under the ground, never to come out into the warm sun again, for that was what he didn't like. The poor little girl was very sad; for now she must say good-bye to the beautiful sun.

"Farewell, bright sun!" she cried, stretching out her arms towards it, and tak-ing another step outside the house; for now the corn had been reaped, and only the dry stubble was left standing. "Farewell, farewell!" she said, and put her arms round a little red flower that grew there. "Give my love to the dear swallow when you see him!"

"Tweet, tweet!" sounded in her ear all at once. She looked up. There was the swallow flying past! As soon as he saw Thumbelina, he was very glad. She told him how unwilling she was to marry the ugly mole, as then she had to live underground where the sun never shone, and she could not help bursting into tears.

"The cold winter is coming now," said the swallow. "I must fly away to warmer lands. Will you come with me? You can sit on my back, and we will fly far away from the ugly mole and his dark house, over the mountains, to the warm countries where the sun shines more brightly than here, where it is always summer, and there are always beautiful flowers. Do come with me, dear little Thumbelina, who saved my life when I lay frozen in the dark tunnel!"

"Yes, I will go with you," said Thumbelina, and got on the swallow's back, with her feet on one side of his outstretched wings. Up he flew into the air, over woods and seas, over the great mountains where the snow is always lying. And if she was cold she crept under his warm feathers, only keeping her little head out

to admire all the beautiful things in the world beneath. At last they came to warm lands; there the sun was brighter, the sky seemed twice as high, and in the hedges hung the finest green and purple grapes; in the woods grew oranges and lemons: the air was scented with myrtle and mint, and on the roads were pretty little children running about and playing with great gorgeous butterflies. But the swallow flew on farther, and it became more and more beautiful. Under the most splendid green trees beside a blue lake stood a glittering white marble castle. Vines hung about the high pillars; there were many swallows' nest, and in one of these lived the swallow who was carrying Thumbelina.

"Here is my house!" said he. "But it won't do for you to live with me; I am not tidy enough to please you. Find a home for yourself in one of the lovely flowers that grow down there; now I will set you down, and you can do whatever you like."

"That will be splendid!" said she, clapping her little hands.

There lay a great white marble column which had fallen to the ground and broken into three pieces, but between these grew the most beautiful white flowers. The swallow flew down with Thumbelina, and set her upon one of the broad leaves. But there, to her astonishment, she found a tiny little man sitting in the middle of the flower, as white and transparent as if he were made of glass; he had the prettiest golden crown on his head, and the most beautiful wings on his shoulders; he himself was no bigger than Thumbelina. He was the spirit of the flower. In each blossom there dwelt a tiny man or woman; but this one was the King over the others.

"How handsome he is!" whispered Thumbelina to the swallow.

The little Prince was very much frightened at the swallow, for in comparison with one so tiny as himself he seemed a giant. But when he saw Thumbelina, he was delighted, for she was the most beautiful girl he had ever seen. So he took his golden crown from off his head and put it on hers, asking her her name, and if she would be his wife, and then she would be Queen of all the flowers. Yes! He was a different kind of husband to the son of the toad and the mole with the black-velvet coat. So she said "Yes" to the noble Prince. And out of each flower came a lady and gentleman, each so tiny and pretty that it was a pleasure to see them. Each brought Thumbelina a present, but the best of all was a beautiful pair of wings which were fastened onto her back, and now she too could fly from flower to flower. They all wished her joy, and the swallow sat above in his nest and sang the wedding march, and that he did as well as he could; but he was sad, because he was very fond of Thumbelina and did not want to be separated from her.

"You shall not be called Thumbelina!" said the spirit of the flower to her. "That is an ugly name, and you are much too pretty for that. We will call you May Blossom."

"Farewell, farewell!" said the little swallow with a heavy heart, and flew away to farther lands, far, far away, right back to Denmark. There he had a little nest above a window, where his wife lived, who can tell fairy stories. "Tweet, tweet!" he sang to her. And that is the way we learnt the whole story.

Goblin Market

by Christina Rossetti

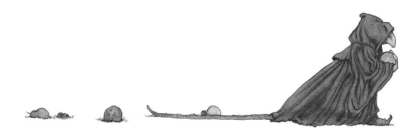

MORNING AND EVENING / Maids heard the goblins cry:
"Come buy our orchard fruits, / Come buy, come buy:
Apples and quinces, / Lemons and oranges,
Plump unpecked cherries, / Melons and raspberries,
Bloom-down-cheeked peaches, / Swart-headed mulberries,
Wild freeborn cranberries, / Crabapples, dewberries,
Pineapples, blackberries, / Apricots, strawberries—
All ripe together / In summer weather—
Morns that pass by, / Fair eves that fly;
Come buy, come buy: / Our grapes fresh from the vine,

Pomegranates full and fine, / Dates and sharp bullaces,

Rare pears and greengages, / Damsons and bilberries,

Taste them and try: / Currants and gooseberries,

Bright firelike barberries, / Figs to fill your mouth,

Citrons from the South, / Sweet to tongue and sound to eye;

Come buy, come buy."

Evening by evening / Among the brookside rushes,

Laura bowed her head to hear, / Lizzie veiled her blushes:

Crouching close together / In the cooling weather,

With clasping arms and cautioning lips, / With tingling cheeks and fingertips.

"Lie close," Laura said, / Pricking up her golden head:

"We must not look at goblin men, / We must not buy their fruits:

Who knows upon what soil they fed / Their hungry thirsty roots?"

"Come buy," call the goblins / Hobbling down the glen.

"Oh," cried Lizzie, "Laura, Laura, / You should not peep at goblin men."

Lizzie covered up her eyes, / Covered close lest they should look;

Laura reared her glossy head, / And whispered like the restless brook:

"Look, Lizzie, look, Lizzie, / Down the glen tramp little men.

One hauls a basket, / One bears a plate,

One lugs a golden dish / Of many pounds weight.

How fair the vine must grow / Whose grapes are so luscious;

How warm the wind must blow / Through those fruit bushes."

"No," said Lizzie: "No, no, no; / Their offers should not charm us,

Their evil gifts would harm us." / She thrust a dimpled finger

In each ear, shut eyes and ran: / Curious Laura chose to linger

Wondering at each merchant man. / One had a cat's face,

One whisked a tail, / One tramped at a rat's pace,

One crawled like a snail, / One like a wombat prowled obtuse and furry,

One like a ratel tumbled hurry skurry. / She heard a voice like voice of doves

Cooing all together: / They sounded kind and full of loves

In the pleasant weather.

Laura stretched her gleaming neck / Like a rush-embedded swan,

Like a lily from the beck, / Like a moonlit poplar branch,

Like a vessel at the launch / When its last restraint is gone.

Backwards up the mossy glen / Turned and trooped the goblin men,

With their shrill repeated cry, / "Come buy, come buy."

When they reached where Laura was / They stood stock still upon the moss,

Leering at each other, / Brother with queer brother;

Signalling each other, / Brother with sly brother.

One set his basket down, / One reared his plate;

One began to weave a crown / Of tendrils, leaves and rough nuts brown

(Men sell not such in any town); / One heaved the golden weight

Of dish and fruit to offer her: / "Come buy, come buy," was still their cry.

Laura stared but did not stir, / Longed but had no money:

The whisk-tailed merchant bade her taste / In tones as smooth as honey,

The cat-faced purr'd, / The rat-paced spoke a word

Of welcome, and the snail-paced even was heard; / One parrot-voiced and jolly

Cried "Pretty Goblin" still for "Pretty Polly"— / One whistled like a bird.

But sweet-tooth Laura spoke in haste: / "Good folk, I have no coin;

To take were to purloin: / I have no copper in my purse,

I have no silver either, / And all my gold is on the furze

That shakes in windy weather / Above the rusty heather."

"You have much gold upon your head," / They answered all together:

"Buy from us with a golden curl." / She clipped a precious golden lock,

She dropped a tear more rare than pearl, / Then sucked their fruit globes fair
      or red:

Sweeter than honey from the rock, / Stronger than man-rejoicing wine,

Clearer than water flowed that juice; / She never tasted such before,

How should it cloy with length of use? / She sucked and sucked and sucked
      the more

Fruits which that unknown orchard bore; / She sucked until her lips were sore;

Then flung the emptied rinds away / But gathered up one kernel-stone,

And knew not was it night or day / As she turned home alone.

Lizzie met her at the gate / Full of wise upbraidings:

"Dear, you should not stay so late, / Twilight is not good for maidens;

Should not loiter in the glen / In the haunts of goblin men.

Do you not remember Jeanie, / How she met them in the moonlight,

Took their gifts both choice and many, / Ate their fruits and wore their
      flowers

Plucked from bowers / Where summer ripens at all hours?

But ever in the noonlight / She pined and pined away;

Sought them by night and day, / Found them no more but dwindled and grew
      gray;

Then fell with the first snow, / While to this day no grass will grow

Where she lies low: / I planted daisies there a year ago

That never blow. / You should not loiter so."

"Nay, hush," said Laura: / "Nay, hush, my sister:
I ate and ate my fill, / Yet my mouth waters still;
Tomorrow night I will / Buy more": and kissed her:
"Have done with sorrow; / I'll bring you plums tomorrow
Fresh on their mother twigs, / Cherries worth getting;
You cannot think what figs / My teeth have met in,
What melons icy-cold / Piled on a dish of gold
Too huge for me to hold, / What peaches with a velvet nap,
Pellucid grapes without one seed: / Odorous indeed must be the mead
Whereon they grow, and pure the wave they drink / With lilies at the brink,
And sugar-sweet their sap."

Golden head by golden head, / Like two pigeons in one nest
Folded in each other's wings, / They lay down in their curtained bed:
Like two blossoms on one stem, / Like two flakes of new-fall'n snow,
Like two wands of ivory / Tipped with gold for awful kings.
Moon and stars gazed in at them, / Wind sang to them lullaby,
Lumbering owls forbore to fly, / Not a bat flapped to and fro
Round their rest: / Cheek to cheek and breast to breast
Locked together in one nest.

Early in the morning / When the first cock crowed his warning,
Neat like bees, as sweet and busy, / Laura rose with Lizzie:
Fetched in honey, milked the cows, / Aired and set to rights the house,
Kneaded cakes of whitest wheat, / Cakes for dainty mouths to eat,
Next churned butter, whipped up cream, / Fed their poultry, sat and sewed;
Talked as modest maidens should: / Lizzie with an open heart,

Laura in an absent dream, / One content, one sick in part;
One warbling for the mere bright day's delight, / One longing for the night.

At length slow evening came: / They went with pitchers to the reedy brook;
Lizzie most placid in her look, / Laura most like a leaping flame.
They drew the gurgling water from its deep; / Lizzie plucked purple and rich
    golden flags,
Then turning homewards said: "The sunset flushes / Those furthest loftiest crags;
Come, Laura, not another maiden lags, / No willful squirrel wags,
The beasts and birds are fast asleep." / But Laura loitered still among the
    rushes.
And said the bank was steep.

And said the hour was early still, / The dew not fall'n, the wind not chill:
Listening ever, but not catching / The customary cry,
"Come buy, come buy," / With its iterated jingle
Of sugar-baited words: / Not for all her watching
Once discerning even one goblin / Racing, whisking, tumbling, hobbling;
Let alone the herds / That used to tramp along the glen,
In groups or single, / Of brisk fruit-merchant men.

Till Lizzie urged, "O Laura, come; / I hear the fruit-call but I dare not look:
You should not loiter longer at this brook: / Come with me home.
The stars rise, the moon bends her arc, / Each glowworm winks her spark,
Let us get home before the night grows dark: / For clouds may gather
Though this is summer weather, / Put out the lights and drench us through;
Then if we lost our way what should we do?"

Laura turned cold as stone / To find her sister heard that cry alone,

That goblin cry, / "Come buy our fruits, come buy."

Must she then buy no more such dainty fruits? / Must she no more that succous pasture find,

Gone deaf and blind? / Her tree of life drooped from the root:

She said not one word in her heart's sore ache; / But peering through the dimness, naught discerning,

Trudged home, her pitcher dripping all the way; / So crept to bed, and lay

Silent till Lizzie slept; / Then sat up in a passionate yearning,

And gnashed her teeth for balked desire, and wept / As if her heart would break.

Day after day, night after night, / Laura kept watch in vain

In sullen silence of exceeding pain. / She never caught again the goblin cry:

"Come buy, come buy"— / She never spied the goblin men

Hawking their fruits along the glen: / But when the noon waxed bright

Her hair grew thin and gray; / She dwindled, as the fair full moon doth turn

To swift decay and burn / Her fire away.

One day remembering her kernel-stone / She set it by a wall that faced the south;

Dewed it with tears, hoped for a root, / Watched for a waxing shoot,

But there came none; / It never saw the sun,

It never felt the trickling moisture run: / While with sunk eyes and faded mouth

She dreamed of melons, as a traveler sees / False waves in desert drought

With shade of leaf-crowned trees, / And burns the thirstier in the sandful breeze.

She no more swept the house, / Tended the fowls or cows,
Fetched honey, kneaded cakes of wheat, / Brought water from the brook:
But sat down listless in the chimney nook / And would not eat.

Tender Lizzie could not bear / To watch her sister's cankerous care
Yet not to share. / She night and morning
Caught the goblins' cry: / "Come buy our orchard fruits,
Come buy, come buy"— / Beside the brook, along the glen,
She heard the tramp of goblin men, / The voice and stir
Poor Laura could not hear; / Longed to buy fruit to comfort her,
But feared to pay too dear. / She thought of Jeanie in her grave,
Who should have been a bride: / But who for joys brides hope to have
Fell sick and died / In her gay prime,
In earliest Winter time, / With the first glazing rime,
With the first snowfall of crisp Winter time.

Till Laura dwindling / Seemed knocking at Death's door:
Then Lizzie weighed no more / Better and worse;
But put a silver penny in her purse, / Kissed Laura, crossed the heath with
    clumps of furze
At twilight, halted by the brook: / And for the first time in her life
Began to listen and look.

Laughed every goblin / When they spied her peeping:
Came towards her hobbling, / Flying, running, leaping,
Puffing and blowing, / Chuckling, clapping, crowing,
Clucking and gobbling, / Mopping and mowing,

Full of airs and graces, / Pulling wry faces,

Demure grimaces, / Catlike and ratlike,

Ratel- and wombatlike, / Snail-paced in a hurry,

Parrot-voiced and whistler, / Helter skelter, hurry skurry,

Chattering like magpies, / Fluttering like pigeons,

Gliding like fishes— / Hugged her and kissed her,

Squeezed and caressed her: / Stretched up their dishes,

Panniers and plates: / "Look at our apples

Russet and dun, / Bob at our cherries,

Bite at our peaches, / Citrons and dates,

Grapes for the asking, / Pears red with basking

Out in the sun, / Plums on their twigs;

Pluck them and suck them. / Pomegranates, figs."

"Good folk," said Lizzie, / Mindful of Jeanie:

"Give me much and many"— / Held out her apron,

Tossed them her penny. / "Nay, take a seat with us,

Honor and eat with us," / They answered grinning:

"Our feast is but beginning. / Night yet is early,

Warm and dew-pearly, / Wakeful and starry:

Such fruits as these / No man can carry;

Half their bloom would fly, / Half their dew would dry,

Half their flavor would pass by. / Sit down and feast with us,

Be welcome guest with us, / Cheer you and rest with us."

"Thank you," said Lizzie: / "But one waits

At home alone for me: / So without further parleying,

If you will not sell me any / Of your fruits though much and many,

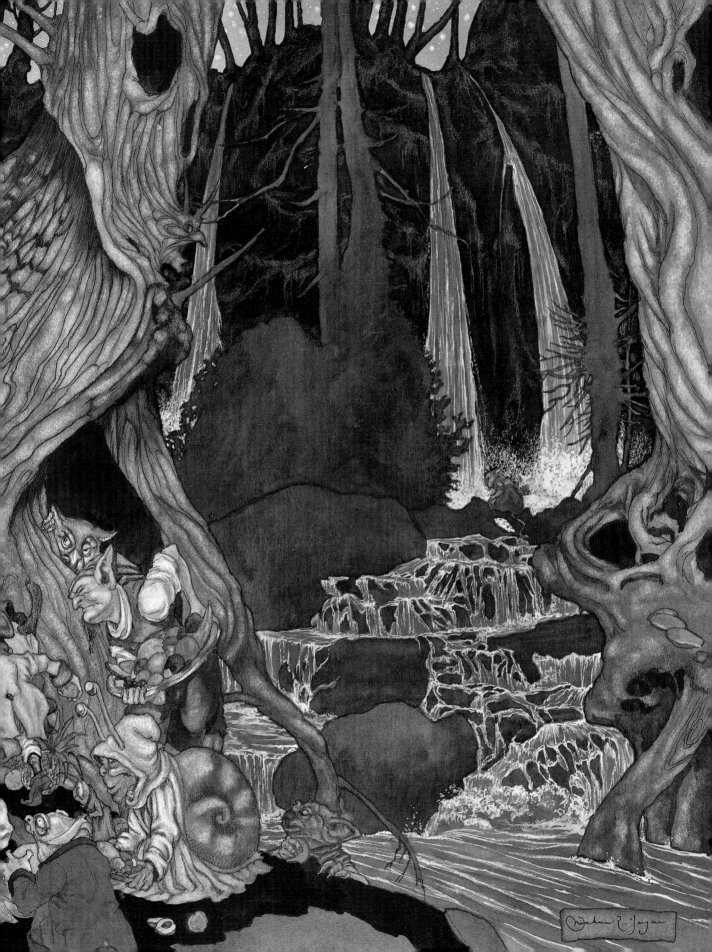

Give me back my silver penny / I tossed you for a fee."
They began to scratch their pates, / No longer wagging, purring,
But visibly demurring, / Grunting and snarling.
One called her proud, / Cross-grained, uncivil;
Their tones waxed loud, / Their looks were evil.
Lashing their tails / They trod and hustled her,
Elbowed and jostled her, / Clawed with their nails,
Barking, mewing, hissing, mocking, / Tore her gown and soiled her stocking,
Twitched her hair out by the roots, / Stamped upon her tender feet,
Held her hands and squeezed their fruits / Against her mouth to make her eat.

White and golden Lizzie stood, / Like a lily in a flood—
Like a rock of blue-veined stone / Lashed by tides obstreperously—
Like a beacon left alone / In a hoary roaring sea,
Sending up a golden fire— / Like a fruit-crowned orange tree
White with blossoms honey-sweet / Sore beset by wasp and bee—
Like a royal virgin town / Topped with gilded dome and spire
Close beleaguered by a fleet / Mad to tug her standard down.

One may lead a horse to water, / Twenty cannot make him drink.
Though the goblins cuffed and caught her, / Coaxed and fought her,
Bullied and besought her, / Scratched her, pinched her black as ink,
Kicked and knocked her, / Mauled and mocked her,
Lizzie uttered not a word; / Would not open lip from lip
Lest they should cram a mouthful in: / But laughed in heart to feel the drip
Of juice that syrupped all her face, / And lodged in dimples of her chin,
And streaked her neck which quaked like curd. / At last the evil people

Worn out by her resistance / Flung back her penny, kicked their fruit
Along whichever road they took, / Not leaving root or stone or shoot;
Some writhed into the ground, / Some dived into the brook
With ring and ripple, / Some scudded on the gale without a sound,
Some vanished in the distance.

In a smart, ache, tingle, / Lizzie went her way;
Knew not was it night or day; / Sprang up the bank, tore thro' the furze,
Threaded corpse and dingle, / And heard her penny jingle
Bouncing in her purse— / Its bounce was music to her ear.
She ran and ran / As if she feared some goblin man
Dogged her with gibe or curse / Or something worse:
But not one goblin skurried after, / Nor was she pricked by fear;
The kind heart made her windy-paced / That urged her home quite out of
    breath with haste
And inward laughter.

She cried, "Laura," up the garden, / "Did you miss me?
Come and kiss me. / Never mind my bruises,
Hug me, kiss me, suck my juices / Squeezed from goblin fruits for you,
Goblin pulp and goblin dew. / Eat me, drink me, love me;
Laura, make much of me: / For your sake I have braved the glen
And had to do with goblin merchant men."

Laura started from her chair, / Flung her arms up in the air,
Clutched her hair: / "Lizzie, Lizzie, have you tasted
For my sake the fruit forbidden? / Must your light like mine be hidden,

Your young life like mine be wasted, / Undone in mine undoing

And ruined in my ruin, / Thirsty, cankered, goblin-ridden?"

She clung about her sister, / Kissed and kissed and kissed her:

Tears once again / Refreshed her shrunken eyes,

Dropping like rain / After long sultry drought;

Shaking with anguish, fear, and pain, / She kissed and kissed her with a hungry
   mouth.

Her lips began to scorch, / That juice was wormwood to her tongue,

She loathed the feast: / Writhing as one possessed she leaped and sung,

Rent all her robe, and wrung / Her hands in lamentable haste,

And beat her breast. / Her locks streamed like the torch

Borne by a racer at full speed, / Or like the mane of horses in their flight,

Or like an eagle when she stems the light / Straight toward the sun,

Or like a caged thing freed, / Or like a flying flag when armies run.

Swift fire spread through her veins, knocked at her heart, / Met the fire
   smoldering there

And overbore its lesser flame; / She gorged on bitterness without a name:

Ah! fool, to choose such part / Of soul-consuming care!

Sense failed in the mortal strife: / Like the watchtower of a town

Which an earthquake shatters down, / Like a lightning-stricken mast,

Like a wind-uprooted tree / Spun about,

Like a foam-topped waterspout / Cast down headlong in the sea,

She fell at last; / Pleasure past and anguish past,

Is it death or is it life?

Life out of death. / That night long Lizzie watched by her,

Counted her pulse's flagging stir, / Felt for her breath,

Held water to her lips, and cooled her face / With tears and fanning leaves:

But when the first birds chirped about their eaves, / And early reapers plodded to the place

Of golden sheaves, / And dew-wet grass

Bowed in the morning winds so brisk to pass, / And new buds with new day

Opened of cuplike lilies on the stream, / Laura awoke as from a dream,

Laughed in the innocent old way, / Hugged Lizzie but not twice or thrice;

Her gleaming locks showed not one thread of gray / Her breath was sweet as May

And light danced in her eyes.

Days, weeks, months, years, / Afterwards, when both were wives

With children of their own; / Their mother-hearts beset with fears,

Their lives bound up in tender lives; / Laura would call the little ones

And tell them of her early prime, / Those pleasant days long gone

Of not-returning time: / Would talk about the haunted glen,

The wicked, quaint fruit-merchant men, / Their fruits like honey to the throat

But poison in the blood; / (Men sell not such in any town:)

Would tell them how her sister stood / In deadly peril to do her good,

And win the fiery antidote: / Then joining hands to little hands

Would bid them cling together, / "For there is no friend like a sister

In calm or stormy weather; / To cheer one on the tedious way,

To fetch one if one goes astray, / To lift one if one totters down,

To strengthen whilst one stands."

The Flower-Babies

by M. Wallace-Dunlop and M. Rivett-Carnac

ONCE UPON A TIME, when fairies danced in the moonlight and the fairy Elves played merry pranks, there used also to be Flower-babies. They were fat chubby small mites, and the flowers loved them dearly, but the naughty Elves thought it great fun to tease them. Flower-babies, you see, were tiny—quite babies—they only knew how to love and to smile, to laugh and to play. They weren't, what the Elves called, useful in the world, they were only just babies. Elves, you see, were older, and could be useful sometimes, when they were good; and very mischievous sometimes when they were naughty.

Now the Flower-baby I am going to tell you about was a Daisy Flower-baby. He lived amongst the daisies. They had given him dear little white wings with a tiny tip of pink underneath to make them pretty. He used to flit about the fields

THE BOOK OF FAIRIES

in the daytime, and his greatest fun was to sit swinging on a daisy. He wasn't very heavy, so when the wind was blowing softly over the grass and all the flowers were bowing and curtseying in the breeze, the daisies used to let him nestle down amidst their white petals. He wasn't the only Flower-baby, there were many of them, but he was a venturesome sprite. Most of the others could only just flitter-flutter from daisy to daisy, and sit swinging and sucking their thumbs, and gurgling at the fun in the world. But Goldy, as he was called, only sucked his thumb sometimes, when he was very puzzled and grave. He was grown too big to suck his thumb, as he could fly now without flitter-fluttering his wings, and could actually pay visits to his friends the daisies far away across the fields. They called him Goldy because his hair was yellow like gold, and curled in a big curl on the top of his head.

One day when he was sitting lazily swinging with his pretty wings spread out, ready to save him from a fall, and gazing about him to see whom he could find to play with, he heard a curious noise—a puffing kind of noise. It puzzled him until he spied two mischievous Elves. They wore tiny red caps, funny yellow-spotted doublets, red hose, and yellow shoes. They had been so quiet, so very quiet, he might have guessed, if he had known more about them, that they were up to mischief. They had crept up to a Daisy and were blowing and puffing out their cheeks and scattering all her pretty white petals. They called it snipping off her kirtle. The poor Daisy could do nothing; they held her fast, and were so much stronger than she was. Soon she was left alone crying over her lost kirtle, while the naughty Elves ran away laughing. Goldy was so distressed he came down and kissed her, and tried to comfort her. He told her not to cry, but the poor little thing could not help crying, for she knew her pretty mantle couldn't be made again quickly, and this made her sad. Goldylocks thought he would go and see if he could find someone to help her, so he flew away to a clump of tall grasses. There he stopped so astonished he quite forgot poor Daisy. What could this great shining thing be in his way? It was spinning round and round, buzzing and fussing and stretching out such queer ugly bits of stalks, thought Goldylocks. He stood with his hands on his little fat knees, gazing at the wonderful monster.

"Flower-baby, Flower-baby, don't stand gaping there, you little silly; help me to get up off my back. Give me a stout blade of grass to catch hold of."

So Goldylocks flew up and sat upon a grass stalk and bent it down. The ugly big things which were the Beetle's feet and hands caught hold of the grass, and as Goldylocks alighted on the ground, the big buzzing grumbling old Beetle pulled himself up off his back, and then fell on his feet, for he was too heavy for the grass to hold him up when once Goldylocks had let go.

"Thank you, Flower-baby," buzzed Mr. Beetle, as he slowly crawled away. "I don't know your name, but next time you want any help, come to me."

It was getting warm, the sun was hot, and Goldylocks had wandered far, so seeing three kind Mother Daisies nodding to him, he flew to them, and sitting

down in their shade he fell fast asleep, with his dear little head on a Daisy bud for a pillow. Now the naughty Elves, after having blown to rags the Daisy's pretty kirtle, had climbed into a May tree, and sitting on the branches amongst the May blossoms, they began to think what more mischief they could do. They sat dangling their legs and swinging their toes for some time. Puck was the one who was always up to most mischief, and at last he said to Robin, "I know what we will do—it will be rare fun—we will go and steal a Flower-baby's wings." "Oh, ho," chuckled Robin, "what fun! They can't fly if we steal their wings. But the little ninnies are so hard to find."

"I know where to look for them," said Puck. "It's just the time of day; it's all cool and breezy up here amongst the May blossoms, but down there in the fields it's very stuffy and we are sure to find one asleep. Now no noise, Robin, don't let me hear you chuckle—follow me, but no noise," and he held up a warning finger.

Now Robin always would chuckle and laugh just when he ought to be quite quiet, and it was most provoking of him. But this time he only smiled all over his face and nodded at Puck. Off they slipped down the May tree, and on tiptoes they began to peer about in the field amongst the daisies.

It *was* very hot, and all the world *was* asleep. There was no one to tell Goldylocks of his danger. He was dreaming he was swinging and that he had

nearly fallen off a very tall daisy when he woke with a start. What was it that had tugged at him and hurt him? He rubbed his sleepy eyes and stood up. His dear pillow the Daisy bud was bending sorrowfully towards him. She whispered to him, "Goldylocks, the naughty Elves have stolen your wings." Goldylocks tried to rise into the air; he couldn't believe Daisy bud. He would fly away, up to Mother Daisy, and swing in her arms. But no—he couldn't rise into the air, he was a poor maimed Flower-baby. He could only stand on his small feet and sob bitterly, "My wings, my dear white wings, they have stolen my wings!" He sobbed and sobbed as if his little heart would break. Far away running as fast as their naughty legs would carry them were Puck and Robin, each carrying a wing and chuckling with delight. They didn't want the wings one bit; they never flew themselves, but it was great fun stealing them away from a stupid Flower-baby. Such a crybaby, too, as it was. "Crybaby, crybaby," they sang mockingly, never thinking how cruel and unkind they were.

But someone heard poor Goldylocks's sobs, and came scurrying up. "Don't cry, don't cry, Flower-baby; why, what's the matter? They have stolen your wings have they, poor little one? Why, you are nearly as badly off as I was when those same tiresome Elves turned me on my back, and left me spinning myself round like a top. But for you, Flower-baby, I might have been still sprawling on my back. Don't cry anymore, but do as I tell you, and I promise to help you," said Mr. Beetle. "You must come with me to my friend the Mermaid who lives in the Silent Pool—but it is a long rough road. You can't go there, now that you have lost your wings, without a little coat. We have to wander through forests—climb mountains, and pass through valleys, and the briers and thorns will hurt you."

Poor Goldylocks, how was he to get a little coat? He had never seen a Flower-baby with such a thing. He looked about with the tears still in his big blue eyes, when a soft voice called to him, "Climb up to me, Goldylocks, don't be afraid. Now that you cannot fly, you must climb, and you must tear off as many strips of my white kirtle as you want. They will show you are my Flower-baby, and nothing will harm you in the forests and the valleys if you wear my livery." So Goldylocks climbed bravely up the daisy stalk—it was so much harder than flying—but at last he got up.

The kind Daisy let him take six big white petals, strips from her white kirtle, and then he slipped quickly down, far quicker than he got up. Then sitting at her feet amongst the clover he made himself a funny little coat. Mr. Beetle, who is very clever with his hands and feet, tied the coat round Goldylocks with a dainty silken cord made of cobwebs borrowed from Dame Spider.

They were soon ready for their journey and started off; Mr. Beetle in front, Goldylocks trotting behind. It was a long long journey, and Flower-baby grew tired and often very frightened, though Mr. Beetle was most kind. The grass was rough to his little feet, the forest of wheat ears they wandered through was very dark, and such strange creatures came round him. When they left the forest of wheat ears—they came to another dark terrible land, full of brambles which tore his pretty white coat, and giant stinging nettles which hurt shockingly—they climbed up big mountains and down into deep valleys, till at last they came to a beautiful pool, shaded by tall trees. Here Mr. Beetle stopped and gave a peculiar drum-drumming call. Poor Goldylocks was so tired and so terrified he sat down and wept bitterly. Then oh! Wonder of wonders, two soft arms gathered him up, a beautiful Mermaid with long dark hair, and lovely eyes the color of the blue water, bent her face over and kissed him. "Tell me all about it, you dear Flower-baby; don't cry, tell me all about it, darling." Then between his sobs, leaning his head on her shoulder, Goldylocks told her all about his lost wings. How he never could fly anymore, how tired it made him coming through those terrible dark forests. How great big creatures with hair on them nipped his legs, shiny round creatures buzzed at him, yellow-legged brown creatures hummed at him, nasty thin-winged monsters stung him. The Mermaid kissed and comforted him. She smiled a little to herself, for she knew the dreadful creature that had so frightened poor Flower-baby was only a tiny field mouse who took his bare toes for

something nice to eat; the shiny creature that buzzed was only one of her friends, a father Beetle going home to his family. Dame Yellow-legs was but a busy Bee, very busy indeed gathering honey; and the winged thin monster was only a Gnat who thought Goldylocks was such a nice soft thing to pinch. One can't help pinching and stinging if one is a Gnat. Poor Goldylocks, it was all "very drefful," as he said, but now he felt safe and happy with these kind arms about him. After he was quite rested, and had had a delightful little bath in the pool, and had floated on a big leaf with his new friend the Mermaid swimming beside him, Goldylocks began to feel that even without his wings he was almost happy. Not quite—for swimming, even though you had a lovely fish's tail all colors of the rainbow like the one Mermaid steered herself by, wasn't quite as nice as flying through the air on your own white wings. Perhaps his kind friend guessed what Goldylocks was feeling, for after she had shown him the fish swimming about in the water, the stately swans with their dear small family gliding through the reeds, and the "silly little ducky dillies with their heads in the lillies and their little toes up in the air," and had made him laugh merrily at them, and had shown him the big bullfrog croaking under the bank with his round staring eyes and solemn face, and the wicked-looking water snake slipping away to hide under a root, she said to him, "Flower-baby, I have shown you many strange things, but my cold Silent Pool is no home for a Flower-baby, so now I will send you to the Flower Fairy and you must tell her about your lost wings, and if you say Mermaid has sent you she will listen."

Goldylocks's eyes grew very big and frightened. "No, no, don't send me through that drefful drefful forest, please, dear Mermaid; I can't fly. Let me stay here and sail on a big leaf; my feet is so tired, so tired."

"But won't you like to go floating away, Flower-baby; won't that be as good as flying?"

"I don't know what floating means," said Goldylocks gravely, shaking his curly head. "I know what flying means. I can fly, but I can't float."

She laughed, and then sinking under the water, she blew and blew, till suddenly there rose from the pool the loveliest round bubble anyone ever saw. The sunlight gleamed upon it; it looked like a great ball of opal, all colors of the rainbow.

Goldylocks fairly danced with joy at the sight of it. "The beautifullest fing" he had ever seen, he said. His friend smiled and said, "Now, Flower-baby, climb up on my shoulder, and sit down on this 'beautifullest fing.'" So Goldylocks, trembling with delight, clambered up on her shoulder, and forgetting even to

kiss his good-bye, sat on the "beautifullest fing" and began to sail away over the stream, and "over the fields and far away." He blew kisses back as fast as he could, then he shouted for joy at feeling himself sailing, sailing away through the air.

How long or how far he sailed he never could say. But at last he floated on to a rosebush, and his fairy Balloon melted away. He found himself kneeling on a rose, while looking down at him was a lovely Fairy. Her golden hair hung down to her waist, her silver robe was embroidered with rose leaves, but oh, joy of joys in Goldylocks's eyes, she had wings, real beautiful wings, blue and silver wings. He wasn't afraid of her—she would know what losing one's wings meant. She would understand how bad it was tottering about on the ground on bare feet, when once one had known what it was to fly. She would know how delightful it was to fly through the air on one's own, very own wings, not floating on a round

slippery air bubble. Swimming was all very well for fishes and frogs, and some birds and mermaids, but the only thing for a Flower-baby was wings.

So kneeling to the Fairy he told her all his long long little story, just as I have tried to tell it, and when he came to the end and said, "Flower-babies can't do without wings," she smiled at him and said, "Quite true, little one. Come and stand here beside me," and then she stooped towards him and fastened on to his shoulders two lovely wings, more beautiful than the white ones he had before, for these were all shot with many colors like the balloon on which he had floated to her feet. When he had kissed her hand in thanks, he flew right away to his dear Daisy Mother to tell her he was safe.

Puck and Robin were very much ashamed of themselves when the Fairy sent for them and made them give up to her the stolen white wings. To punish them for being cruel and unkind, she made them each wear, for several days, a pair of cockchafer's wings, and wouldn't allow them to use their legs. As they were very nimble on their feet, and extremely awkward with their wings, every bird, bat, and insect, mocked at them and laughed at them. They soon found that being teased was not quite so amusing after all. When the Fairy let them put off their wings and use their legs again, they didn't go about any longer worrying Flower-babies or making themselves disagreeable as before.

Fairer-than-a-Fairy

by Charlotte-Rose Caumont de la Force

ONCE THERE LIVED a king who had no children for many years after his marriage. At length heaven granted him a daughter of such remarkable beauty that he could think of no name so appropriate for her as "Fairer-than-a-Fairy."

It never occurred to the good-natured monarch that such a name was certain to call down the hatred and jealousy of the fairies in a body on the child, but this was what happened. No sooner had they heard of this presumptuous name than they resolved to gain possession of her who bore it, and either to torment her cruelly, or at least to conceal her from the eyes of all men.

The eldest of their tribe was entrusted to carry out their revenge. This Fairy was named Lagree; she was so old that she only had one eye and one tooth left, and even these poor remains she had to keep all night in a strengthening liquid. She was also so spiteful that she gladly devoted all her time to carrying out all the mean or ill-natured tricks of the whole body of fairies.

With her large experience, added to her native spite, she found but little difficulty in carrying off Fairer-than-a-Fairy. The poor child, who was only seven years old, nearly died of fear on finding herself in the power of this hideous creature. However, when after an hour's journey underground she found herself in a splendid palace with lovely gardens, she felt a little reassured, and was further cheered when she discovered that her pet cat and dog had followed her.

The old Fairy led her to a pretty room which she said should be hers, at the same time giving her the strictest orders never to let out the fire which was burning brightly in the grate. She then gave two glass bottles into the Princess's charge, desiring her to take the greatest care of them, and having enforced her orders with the most awful threats in case of disobedience, she vanished, leaving the little girl at liberty to explore the palace and grounds and a good deal relieved at having only two apparently easy tasks set her.

Several years passed, during which time the Princess grew accustomed to her lonely life, obeyed the Fairy's orders, and by degrees forgot all about the court of the King her father.

One day, whilst passing near a fountain in the garden, she noticed that the sun's rays fell on the water in such a manner as to produce a brilliant rainbow. She stood still to admire it, when, to her great surprise, she heard a voice addressing her which seemed to come from the center of its rays. The voice was that of a young man, and its sweetness of tone and the agreeable things it uttered led one to infer that its owner must be equally charming; but this had to be a mere matter of fancy, for no one was visible.

The beautiful Rainbow informed Fairer-than-a-Fairy that he was young, the son of a powerful king, and that the Fairy, Lagree, who owed his parents a grudge, had revenged herself by depriving him of his natural shape for some years; that she had imprisoned him in the palace, where he had found his confinement hard to bear for some time, but now, he owned, he no longer sighed for freedom since he had seen and learned to love Fairer-than-a-Fairy.

He added many other tender speeches to this declaration, and the Princess, to whom such remarks were a new experience, could not help feeling pleased and touched by his attentions.

The Prince could only appear or speak under the form of a Rainbow, and it was therefore necessary that the sun should shine on water so as to enable the rays to form themselves.

Fairer-than-a-Fairy lost no moment in which she could meet her lover, and they enjoyed many long and interesting interviews. One day, however, their conversation became so absorbing and time passed so quickly that the Princess forgot to attend to the fire, and it went out. Lagree, on her return, soon found out the neglect, and seemed only too pleased to have the opportunity of showing her spite to her lovely prisoner. She ordered Fairer-than-a-Fairy to start next day at dawn to ask Locrinos for fire with which to relight the one she had allowed to go out.

Now this Locrinos was a cruel monster who devoured everyone he came across, and especially enjoyed a chance of catching and eating any young girls. Our heroine obeyed with great sweetness, and without having been able to take leave of her lover she set off to go to Locrinos as to certain death. As she was crossing a wood a bird sang to her to pick up a shining pebble which she would find in a fountain close by, and to use it when needed. She took the bird's advice, and in due time arrived at the house of Locrinos. Luckily she only found his wife at home, who was much struck by the Princess's youth and beauty and sweet gentle manners, and still further impressed by the present of the shining pebble.

She readily let Fairer-than-a-Fairy have the fire, and in return for the stone she gave her another, which, she said, might prove useful someday. Then she sent her away without doing her any harm.

Lagree was as much surprised as displeased at the happy result of this expedition, and Fairer-than-a-Fairy waited anxiously for an opportunity of meeting Prince Rainbow and telling him her adventures. She found, however, that he had already been told all about them by a Fairy who protected him, and to whom he was related.

The dread of fresh dangers to his beloved Princess made him devise some more convenient way of meeting than by the garden fountain, and Fairer-than-a-Fairy carried out his plan daily with entire success. Every morning she placed a large basin full of water on her windowsill, and as soon as the sun's rays fell on the water the Rainbow appeared as clearly as it had ever done in the fountain. By this means they were able to meet without losing sight of the fire or of the two bottles in which the old Fairy kept her eye and her tooth at night, and for some time the lovers enjoyed every hour of sunshine together.

One day Prince Rainbow appeared in the depths of woe. He had just heard that he was to be banished from this lovely spot, but he had no idea where he was to go. The poor young couple were in despair, and only parted with the last ray of sunshine, and in hopes of meeting next morning. Alas! Next day was dark and gloomy, and it was only late in the afternoon that the sun broke through the clouds for a few minutes.

Fairer-than-a-Fairy eagerly ran to the window, but in her haste she upset the basin, and spilt all the water with which she had carefully filled it overnight. No other water was at hand except that in the two bottles. It was the only chance of seeing her lover before they were separated, and she did not hesitate to break the bottles and pour their contents into the basin, when the Rainbow appeared at once. Their farewells were full of tenderness; the Prince made the most ardent and sincere protestations, and promised to neglect nothing which might help to deliver his dear Fairer-than-a-Fairy from her captivity, and implored her to consent to their marriage as soon as they should both be free. The Princess, on her side, vowed to have no other husband, and declared herself willing to brave death itself in order to rejoin him.

They were not allowed much time for their adieus; the Rainbow vanished, and the Princess, resolved to run all risks, started off at once, taking nothing with her but her dog, her cat, a sprig of myrtle, and the stone which the wife of Locrinos gave her.

When Lagree became aware of her prisoner's flight she was furious, and set off at full speed in pursuit. She overtook her just as the poor girl, overcome by fatigue, had lain down to rest in a cave which the stone had formed itself into to shelter her. The little dog who was watching her mistress promptly flew at Lagree and bit her so severely that she stumbled against a corner of the cave and broke off her only tooth. Before she had recovered from the pain and rage this caused her, the Princess had time to escape, and was some way on her road. Fear gave her strength for some time, but at last she could go no further, and sank down to rest. As she did so, the sprig of myrtle she carried touched the ground, and immediately a green and shady bower sprang up round her, in which she hoped to sleep in peace.

But Legree had not given up her pursuit, and arrived just as Fairer-than-a-Fairy had fallen fast asleep. This time she made sure of catching her victim, but the cat spied her out, and, springing from one of the boughs of the arbor she flew at Legree's face and tore out her only eye, thus delivering the Princess forever from her persecutor.

One might have thought that all would now be well, but no sooner had Lagree been put to flight than our heroine was overwhelmed with hunger and thirst. She felt as though she should certainly expire, and it was with some difficulty that she dragged herself as far as a pretty little green and white house, which stood at no great distance. Here she was received by a beautiful lady dressed in green and white to match the house, which apparently belonged to her, and of which she seemed the only inhabitant.

She greeted the fainting Princess most kindly, gave her an excellent supper, and after a long night's rest in a delightful bed told her that after many troubles she should finally attain her desire.

As the green and white lady took leave of the Princess she gave her a nut, desiring her only to open it in the most urgent need.

After a long and tiring journey Fairer-than-a-Fairy was once more received in a house, and by a lady exactly like the one she had quit. Here again she received a present with the same injunctions, but instead of a nut this lady gave her a golden pomegranate. The mournful Princess had to continue her weary way, and after many troubles and hardships she again found rest and shelter in a third house exactly similar to the two others.

These houses belonged to three sisters, all endowed with fairy gifts, and all so alike in mind and person that they wished their houses and garments to be equally alike. Their occupation consisted in helping those in misfortune, and they were as gentle and benevolent as Legree had been cruel and spiteful.

The third Fairy comforted the poor traveler, begged her not to lose heart, and assured her that her troubles should be rewarded. She accompanied her advice by the gift of a crystal smelling-bottle, with strict orders only to open it in case of urgent need. Fairer-than-a-Fairy thanked her warmly, and resumed her way cheered by pleasant thoughts.

After a time her road led through a wood, full of soft airs and sweet odors, and before she had gone a hundred yards she saw a wonderful silver Castle suspended by strong silver chains to four of the largest trees. It was so perfectly hung that a gentle breeze rocked it sufficiently to send you pleasantly to sleep.

Fairer-than-a-Fairy felt a strong desire to enter this Castle, but besides being hung a little above the ground there seemed to be neither doors nor windows. She had no doubt (though really I cannot think why) that the moment had come in which to use the nut which had been given her. She opened it, and out came a diminutive hall porter at whose belt hung a tiny chain, at the end of which was a golden key half as long as the smallest pin you ever saw.

The Princess climbed up one of the silver chains, holding in her hand the little porter who, in spite of his minute size, opened a secret door with his golden key and let her in. She entered a magnificent room which appeared to occupy the entire Castle, and which was lighted by gold and jeweled stars in the ceiling. In the midst of this room stood a couch, draped with curtains of all the colors of the rainbow, and suspended by golden cords so that it swayed with the Castle in a manner which rocked its occupant delightfully to sleep.

On this elegant couch lay Prince Rainbow, looking more beautiful than ever, and sunk in profound slumber, in which he had been held ever since his disappearance.

Fairy-than-a-Fairy, who now saw him for the first time in his real shape, hardly dared to gaze at him, fearing lest his appearance might not be in keeping with the voice and language which had won her heart. At the same time she could not help feeling rather hurt at the apparent indifference with which she was received.

She related all the dangers and difficulties she had gone through, and though she repeated the story twenty times in a loud clear voice, the Prince slept on and took no heed. She then had recourse to the golden pomegranate, and on opening it found that all the seeds were as many little violins which flew up in the vaulted roof and at once began playing melodiously.

The Prince was not completely roused, but he opened his eyes a little and looked all the handsomer.

Impatient at not being recognized, Fairer-than-a-Fairy now drew out her third present, and on opening the crystal scent-bottle a little siren flew out, who silenced the violins and then sang close to the Prince's ear the story of all his lady love had suffered in her search for him. She added some gentle reproaches to her tale, but before she had got far he was wide awake, and transported with joy threw himself at the Princess's feet. At the same moment the walls of the room expanded and opened out, revealing a golden throne covered with jewels. A magnificent Court now began to assemble, and at the same time several elegant carriages filled with ladies in magnificent dresses drove up. In the first and most splendid of these carriages sat Prince Rainbow's mother. She fondly embraced her son, after which she informed him that his father had been dead for some years, that the anger of the Fairies was at length appeased, and that he might return in peace to reign over his people, who were longing for his presence.

The court received the new King with joyful acclamations which would have delighted him at any other time, but all his thoughts were full of Fairer-than-a-Fairy. He was just about to present her to his mother and the Court, feeling sure that her charms would win all hearts, when the three green and white sisters appeared.

They declared the secret of Fairy-than-a-Fairy's royal birth, and the Queen taking the two lovers in her carriage set off with them for the capital of the kingdom.

Here they were received with tumultuous joy. The wedding was celebrated without delay, and succeeding years diminished neither the virtues, beauty, nor the mutual affection of King Rainbow and his Queen, Fairer-than-a-Fairy.

The Goodwife's Midnight Labors

retold by Elizabeth Grierson

THERE WAS ONCE a goodwife who was so stirring and notable that she would rest neither by night nor by day. In the daytime when the meals were cooked and the house was redded up and the animals fed she would wander about and gather wisps of wool caught on the brambles, and at night she would card them and spin them and weave them, and make them up into coats for her man and the bairns. But it was weary work; and one night, as she sat up long after everyone was abed, she threw down her spindle and cried out: "Ahone, but I'm weary. A body may card, card, card, spin, spin, spin, all day and all night, and what thanks will she get, or help? I'm sure I'd be willing enough to take help from any living thing."

It was a foolish thing to say, for trouble may always be had for the asking. The words were hardly out of her mouth when there was a knock on the door.

The goodwife went to open it, and outside stood the queerest wee body with a green gown and a white mutch.

"Save us! Who's there?" said the goodwife.

"Tall Quarry, goodwife," said the old woman. "While I hae ye'll get." And she crossed over to the fire and began to card. There was another knock, and the goodwife cried out: "Who's there?"

"Tall Quarry," said another voice. "While I hae ye'll get." And another old woman like the first came in and began to spin. She had hardly started when a third came, who made the same reply and settled down to weave. The goodwife was watching them in some alarm when the door opened again, and a fairy boy came in, followed by such a swarm that you might have thought that all the fairies in Scotland were there. They carded and spun and wove and boiled the cloth in the fulling pot like mad; and the house was full of the racket of them. For if they had hands they had mouths as well, and all the time they worked they clamored for food. The goodwife ran to bake bannocks for them, but as fast as one was cooked it was snatched off the fire, and still the clamor went on. At length the goodwife left her cookery and ran to ask her husband what she should do. To her horror he lay like a log, and, shake him as she might, she could not waken him. It was plain that he was bewitched. The goodwife was at her wit's end until she thought of consulting a Wise Man who lived near. She pulled her shawl over her head and hurried out to his house. Luckily the Wise Man was but just gone to bed; and he thrust his head out of the window and listened to her story.

"Aweel, there's but one thing to do," he said. "If the Good Neighbors have been fulling throw the fulling water over him and he'll maybe waken. But you must get them out from the house first, and syne keep them out. Go back, and as ye come up to the door cry out: 'The Burg Hill is afire!' That's where they stay, ye ken. And they'll run out to save what they value most. But mind this, it's of no use to turn them out if ye canna keep them out; so undo all that they've done, or the things they have worked on will rise and open to them."

The goodwife thanked the Wise Man, and ran as fast as she could to her own house. She flung the door open and cried out: "The Burg Hill's afire! The Burg Hill's afire!"

At once there was a great clatter and clamor, and the Good People swarmed past her, each crying out the name of his most prized possession. No sooner had they gone than the goodwife slammed to the door, and began to destroy every trace of their work. She pulled the fulling water off the fire and tore the web of cloth, loosed the band of the spinning wheel and turned the distaff upside down, burnt the carded wool and put the cardens in the press. She had barely finished when the fairies knocked at the door.

"Let us in, goodwife. While we get ye'll hae."

"That I'll not," said the goodwife. "Once is enough for this while."

"Wheel that we spun on," cried the fairies through the keyhole. "Rise and let us in."

A squeaking, wheezy voice came from the spinning wheel. "I canna let ye in, for the goodwife 's lowsed my band."

"Cardens, cardens, rise and let us in," said the fairies again, and a small hoarse voice said: "Hoo can I rise when she's locked me in the press and pit ma wool on the fire?"

"Loom that we worked on, rise up and let us in," they cried again, and a soft, tongueless voice said: "Hoo can ye ask me tae rise when my web's torn and my heddle's lying on the ground?"

At that the goodwife laughed, and the fairies cried out: "Bannocks that we baked, rise up and let us in."

The goodwife gave a shriek, for she had forgotten the bannocks. There was one little barley bannock cooking on the fire, the last the fairies had set there, and it got up and began to roll towards the door. But the goodwife nipped it between her finger and thumb, and it fell to the ground, for it was but half baked. At that the fairies cried out tauntingly:

"Aha, goodwife, look till yir man! Ye'll no get yir man to waken!"

Sure enough, as they cried out the goodman began to toss and mutter like one mad. The goodwife wrung her hands again; then she remembered the Wise Man's counsel, and ran to fetch the fulling water. As she dashed the water over her husband the fairies all about the house set up a dismal cry and fled, and the man wakened as well as he had ever been. As for the goodwife, she was careful, after this, never to wish for a thing unless she knew what she was wishing for.

The Brownie o' Ferne-Den

retold by Virginia Haviland

MANY BROWNIES there have been in Scotland. And one of them was known as "the Brownie o' Ferne-Den."

Now Ferne-Den was a farmhouse. It had its name from the glen, or "den," near which it stood, for anyone who wished to reach the farm had to pass through this glen.

All around, the country folk believed that a brownie lived in the glen. Never would he appear to anyone in the daytime, but it was said he was sometimes seen at night. He would steal about like an ungainly shadow, moving from tree to tree to keep from being seen. And he never did harm to anybody, this Brownie o' Ferne-Den.

Indeed, like all good brownies that are properly treated and let alone, the Brownie o' Ferne-Den was always on the lookout to do a good turn to those in need of his help.

The farmer of Ferne-Den did not know what he would ever do without this brownie. If he had any farmwork to be finished in a hurry, it would be done. The brownie would thrash his grain, and winnow it, and tie it up into bags. He would cut the turnips, too. And for the farmer's wife he would wash the clothes, work the churn, or weed the garden.

All that the farmer and his wife had to do was to leave open the door of the barn, or the turnip shed, or the milk house, when they went to bed. And they must put down a bowl of new milk on the doorstep for the brownie's supper. When they woke the next morning the bowl would be empty, and the job would be finished better than if it had been done by mortal hands.

Now all of this should have proved how gentle and kindly this brownie was. But all the workers on the farm had a fear of him. They would go miles around in the dark, coming home from kirk on the Sunday or market on Market Day, to avoid passing through the brownie's glen and catching a sight of him.

The farmer's lady herself was so good and gentle a housewife that she felt no fear of the brownie. When the brownie's supper was to be left outside, it was she who would fill his bowl with the richest milk, and she would add a good spoonful of cream to it, too.

"Aye," said she, "he works hard for us, right enough, and never asks for wages. Well does he deserve the very best meal we can set out for him."

One night this gentle lady was taken ill, and everyone was afraid she might die. Her husband took it hard, indeed, and so, too, did her servants. Such a good mistress she had ever been to them that they loved her as if she were their mother. Now she was that bad that they were all for sending for the old nurse who lived miles off on the other side of the glen.

Who was to go to fetch her? That was the question. It was black midnight when the lady fell ill, and the only way to the old nurse's house lay straight through the glen. Whoever traveled that road would run the risk of meeting the brownie.

The farmer himself would have gone, well enough, but he dared not leave his wife. As for the timid servants, they stood about in the kitchen, each telling the other that he was the one to go. And no one of them offered to go himself.

Little did they know that the brownie, who was the very cause of their fear, was hiding only a few feet away from them, in the entry outside the kitchen. There he crouched, a queer wee man, all covered with hair. He had a long beard and red-rimmed eyes. His broad feet were webbed like those of a duck, and his long arms touched the ground, even when he stood up.

The brownie, with his face all anxious, tried to hear their words. He had come as usual from his home in the glen to see if there were any work for him to do, and to look for his bowl of milk. He knew fine that something now was wrong inside the farmhouse. Usually, at this late hour, all was dark and still, but here were the windows lit up and the door wide open.

The brownie learned from the servants' jabber that his kind mistress, whom he loved so dearly, was deathly ill. He became sad, indeed. And when he found that the silly servants were so full of their fears that they dared not go for the nurse, his anger grew far greater than their fear.

"Fools and idiots!" he muttered, stamping his queer flat feet. "They talk as if a brownie would take a bite right off them. If the like of them only knew the bother they give me to keep out of their way, they would not be so silly. Aye, by my troth, if they keep on like this, the bonny lady will die amongst their fingers. It strikes me that brownie must away, himself, for the nurse."

Up he reached with his hand and took down from its peg on the wall the farmer's great dark cloak. Hiding under it, he hurried out to the stable, to saddle and bridle the farmer's fleetest horse.

When the last buckle was fastened, the brownie led the horse out of the stable and scrambled up onto its back. "If ever you have flown fast, fly fast now," begged the brownie.

It was as if the horse understood the brownie. It gave a quick whinny, pricked up its ears, and darted into the darkness like an arrow from a bow.

In less time than the distance had ever been traveled before, the brownie came to the old woman's cottage.

Now the nurse, of course, was in bed asleep. The brownie had to rap sharply on her window. When she rose and put her old face close to the glass to ask who was there, he told her quickly why he had come at this late hour.

"You must come with me, goodwife, and that at once," he commanded in a deep voice, "if the lady of Ferne-Den is to be saved. There is no one to nurse her at the farm save the lot of silly servants."

"Aye, but how shall I get there? Have they sent a cart for me?" asked the old woman. As far as she could see, there was nothing at the door save the horse and its rider.

"Nay, they have sent no cart," replied the brownie. "You must just climb up behind me on the saddle, and hang on tight. I'll promise to land you at Ferne-Den safe and sound."

The brownie's voice was so commanding that the old woman dared not refuse to do as she was bid. Besides, she had often ridden thus on a horse when she was a lassie. So, she made haste to dress herself and soon unlocked her door. She climbed up behind the stranger, who was almost hidden in his dark cloak. She clasped him tightly and they were off.

Not a word was spoken between them till they neared the glen. Then the old woman began to feel her courage giving way. "Do you think we might meet the brownie?" she asked timidly. "I have no fancy to run the risk, for folk say that he is an unchancy creature."

The brownie gave his own odd laugh. "Keep up your heart, and cease talking foolishly," he said. "I promise you there will be naught uglier this night than the man you ride behind."

"Oh, good on you, then, I'm fine and safe," said the old woman. "I have not seen your face, but I warrant you are a true man, for the care you have taken of the poor lady of Ferne-Den."

She fell into silence again till they had passed through the glen and the good horse had turned into the farmyard. The brownie now slid to the ground. Turning around, he carefully lifted her down with his long, strong arms. But—as he did so, the cloak slipped off him. She saw his strange, short body.

"In all the world, what kind of man are you?" the old woman asked. She peered into his face in the graying light of morning. "What makes your eyes so big? And what have you done to your feet? They are more like duck's webs than aught else."

The queer little brownie laughed. "I've walked many a mile without a horse to help me, and I've heard it said that too much walking makes the feet unshapely.

"But waste no time in talking now, good dame. Go into the house. And if anyone asks who brought you hither so quickly, tell them—they who fear the brownie—that there was a lack of men to help the good mistress. You had to ride here behind the Brownie o' Ferne-Den."

The Fairies

by William Allingham

Up the airy mountain,
  Down the rushy glen,
We daren't go a-hunting
  For fear of little men;
Wee folk, good folk,
  Trooping all together;
Green jacket, red cap,
  And white owl's feather!

Down along the rocky shore
Some make their home,
They live on crispy pancakes
Of yellow tide foam;

Some in the reeds
    Of the black mountain lake,
With frogs for their watchdogs,
    All night awake.

High on the hilltop
    The old King sits;
He is now so old and gray
    He's nigh lost his wits.

With a bridge of white mist
    Columbkill he crosses,
On his stately journeys
    From Slieveleague to Rosses;
Or going up with music
    On cold starry nights,
To sup with the Queen
    Of the gay Northern Lights.

They stole little Bridget
    For seven years long;
When she came down again
    Her friends were all gone.
They took her lightly back,
    Between the night and morrow,
They thought that she was fast asleep,
    But she was dead with sorrow.

They have kept her ever since
    Deep within the lake,
On a bed of flag-leaves,
    Watching till she wake.

By the craggy hillside,
    Through the mosses bare,
They have planted thorn trees
    For pleasure here and there.

Is any man so daring
    As dig them up in spite,
He shall find their sharpest thorns
    In his bed at night.

Up the airy mountain,
    Down the rushy glen,
We daren't go ahunting
    For fear of little men;
Wee folk, good folk,
    Trooping all together;
Green jacket, red cap,
    And white owl's feather!

More about Fairies

FOR THOUSANDS OF YEARS, people have told stories and sung songs about the magical creatures some think share the earth with us. The creatures we call fairies include brownies, elves, and other "little folk."

Fairy stories were not originally meant for children. Scottish adults told "The Brownie o' Ferne Den" aloud to each other. Mademoiselle de la Force wrote "Fairer-than-a-Fairy" for other wealthy French ladies at the end of the 1600s. Charles Perrault's "Cinderella," "The Sleeping Beauty," and "Puss in Boots" were enjoyed by the same audience. By the 1800s, writers like Hans Christian Andersen were writing stories meant specifically for children—but adults remained interested in fairies, too. Soon after cameras were invented, one man claimed to have photographed tiny winged fairies in his garden. That would have been a dangerous act: Anyone who knows fairy lore understands that fairies generally prefer not to be looked at.

The word *fairy* meant a place before it meant a kind of creature. Poets and storytellers would say that something was "of faerie"—from the land of fairy—meaning that it was magical or enchanted. Only later did it mean the inhabitants of that land. In the nineteenth century, wealthy landowners took over many small farms in Scotland and Ireland to graze their vast herds of sheep. Forced to move to towns or cities, people told fewer of the old stories. "The sheep at the fairies," the farmers used to say.

But people still tell the old stories about fairies and continue to make up new ones. Fairies may not be easy to live with, but we don't want to live without them either. A world without magic and danger would be boring. Stories of fairies remind us how unpredictable and interesting the world really is. And they remind us that we must have times of struggle before we can have happy endings.

Notes

Lock-out Time, excerpted from
  Peter Pan in Kensington Gardens
by J. M. Barrie

"Lock-out Time" is a story from *Peter Pan in Kensington Gardens.* This is not the book about Peter Pan and Wendy, but a series of stories about Peter and the fairies. Barrie made them up for the sons of a friend. One of the boys, named David, appears in this story.

Kensington Gardens is a real park in London where Barrie took the boys to play, and all the places in the story are real. A river flows through the gardens, and in the river sits Bird Island. There, says Barrie, all the birds are born that will later become children. In another part of the book, Barrie tells us that Peter Pan can talk to the fairies because he flew out of his nursery window and back to the gardens when he was only seven days old—before he had forgotten how to speak the fairy language. Other children forget.

Flower fairies first appeared in English literature four hundred years ago, in the court of the fairy king and queen. They love to dance and are usually invisible to human beings. Many stories of fairies tell of what happens when fairies and mortals meet each other, but Barrie is more interested in what the fairies do when we are not watching.

Thumbelina
by Hans Christian Andersen

Andersen liked to write stories about misfit characters who suffer hardships before discovering who they are and where they fit in. Thumbelina, a lost flower fairy, is one of them. So are the Ugly Duckling and the Little Mermaid, two of Andersen's best-loved characters.

Andersen understood misfits. He was a tall, awkward, funny-looking boy who didn't want to be a shoemaker like his father, or do any of the other jobs that a poor Danish boy could do in the early 1800s. Instead, he left home at the age of fourteen. Through hard work, talent, luck, and a refusal to give up, he became famous. "My life is a fairy story," he liked to say.

Often Andersen retold stories he had heard as a child, but Thumbelina is his own creation. He published her story in 1835 in a small pamphlet and then reprinted it in *Eventyr, Fortalte for Børn* (*Fairy Tales, Told for Children*). In Danish, her name was Tommelise. This translation is from *The Yellow Fairy Book*, published by Andrew Lang in 1894.

Goblin Market
by Christina Rossetti

Christina Rossetti's goblins are particularly nasty creatures. Fairies do not usually go to so much trouble to hurt people. Their markets are private, but they harm only people who interrupt them when they are busy.

Rossetti makes her poem a kind of enchantment. Like Laura, we are trapped, dizzy and half-hypnotized. The words become a kind of magic spell, making it easy to understand why Laura was tempted by the goblins' sales pitch.

Little of this poem is based on fairy lore, but one part of the story is traditional: People who stumble into the power of the fairies often need to be rescued by someone who is very loving and brave. As the poet says, Laura is lucky to have such a good sister.

The Flower-Babies
by M. Wallace-Dunlop and M. Rivett-Carnac

The elves, Puck and Robin, are both named for one famous fairy: Robin Goodfellow, nicknamed Puck. He appears in Shakespeare's *A Midsummer Night's Dream* and in other English literature and loves to play tricks. In this story the elves act less like fairies than like children teasing a younger sibling, or like bullies on a playground.

In 1899, when this story was first published, children's books were supposed to teach children how to behave. This is a story about a flower-baby's adventures, and it is rich with fairy creatures, including elves, flower fairies, and a mermaid, but it is also a story that says "Don't tease!"

Fairer-than-a-Fairy
by Charlotte-Rose Caumont de la Force

In the 1600s, wealthy French women began making up stories of magic and romance and telling them to one another. Later, some of the tales were written down and published. A few of the stories, like "Little Red Riding Hood," were about children. Most told of young men and women who had to suffer but behave nobly before they could marry and live happily ever after. Some of these stories didn't even have fairies in them, but "fairy tales" was what they were called: *contes de fées. Fée* (pronounced *fay*) is the French word for *fairy.*

In "Fairer-than-a-Fairy," the fairy Lagree might remind us of the fairy who puts a curse on Sleeping Beauty, punishing the girl because her parents forget to invite the fairy to the child's christening. Mean fairies don't seem to mind blaming children for their parents' mistakes—as Lagree does in this story of a beautiful girl with an unlucky name.

The Goodwife's Midnight Labors
retold by Elizabeth Grierson

"Trouble may always be had for the asking," says the storyteller, and that is certainly true for the hardworking heroine of this tale. One careless wish lands her with a whole houseful of fairies. They pretend to be helping her, but they are out of control.

This Scottish folktale is full of traditional beliefs about fairies: They wear green, a color many British people avoided for fear of bad luck; their work in the woman's house gives them power over her, which is why she must undo the work to keep them out; and the wise man who helps the woman knows not to call the fairies by name—instead he calls them the "good neighbors," the name people felt Scottish and Irish fairies sometimes preferred to be known by. The wise man also knows how to wake the woman's husband out of his enchanted sleep: Throw the fulling water on him. "Fulling" the woolen cloth—boiling it until it shrank—made it heavier and warmer.

The Brownie o' Ferne-Den
retold by Virginia Haviland

Fairies can be dangerously unpredictable, but brownies can generally be counted on. They will often attach themselves to a house or farm and remain loyal to the people who live there. If treated properly, they help with the chores each night.

The woman in this Scottish folktale knows just how to stay on good terms with her resident brownie: She leaves it a bowl of rich milk and cream each night, but she doesn't give it directly to the brownie. Instead she leaves it where the brownie can find it. The food left for a brownie is never supposed to be payment. It's more like a thank-you present. In folktales, people who hand food to the brownie or leave it a suit of clothing usually find themselves deserted.

In the world of fairy tales, a pretty face may prove goodness within, but other times it is a disguise. This story reminds us to judge creatures by their actions, not their looks. The ugly, strangely shaped little brownie is kind and loyal. It is the people who fear him who look silly, and the brownie quite rightly thinks them fools and cowards.

The Fairies
by William Allingham

Allingham's fairies, dressed in green jackets and red caps, are the fairies of Irish tradition. He includes other fairy lore, too. He avoids saying the name "fairies," except in his title, calling them by the names people think they prefer. But like the "good neighbors" in "The Goodwife's Midnight Labors," these fairies aren't really very good or nice. In one old Scottish rhyme, the fairies say that if we call them good neighbors, then that's what they'll be. Well, maybe. It seems to depend on what kind of mood they are in.

Bridget, stolen away by the fairies, doesn't find them good, especially since she suffers a common problem of people taken by the fairies: Time in fairyland is not the same as human time. Someone may spend seven years with the fairies—or even one night—and return to find that a hundred years have passed.

Fairies may not be nice by human standards, but the poet—like most of us— clearly likes the idea of living in a world populated by these tough, magic little creatures.